Date Due

JE 20 '89	JY 3 '91	NOV 12 [illegible]	
JY 14 '89	SE 18 '91	NOV 23 '9[illegible]	
JY 20 '89	JY 20 '92	JUL 15 '98	
JY 28 '89	AG 14 '92	SEP 28 '98	
AG 21 '89	AP 16 '93	DE 28 [illegible]	
MY 5 '90		JY 15 '02	
JE 19 '90	JE 7 '93	JY 23 '07	
JY 11 '90	JY 8 '93	JY 07 [illegible]	
AG 20 '90	JY 29 '93	AP 18 '13	
SE 18 '90	JUN 27 '9[illegible]	AG 01 '13	
DE 15 '90	JUL 27 '94		
JA 23 '91	SEP 21 '9[illegible]		

Gordon, Sharon
Mike's first
haircut

A First-Start Easy Reader

This easy reader contains only 56 different words, repeated often to help the young reader develop word recognition and interest in reading.

Basic word list for *Mike's First Haircut*

a
and
asks
be
but
cannot
cut
day
does
ears
every
eyes
for
grows
hair
haircut
hear
his
how
I
is
it
like
long
longer
look
looks
man
me
Mike
Mike's
Mother
my
no
not
oh
over
please
rather
really
says
see
she
short
soon
that
the
this
time
too
was
who
what
will
would
your

Mike's First Haircut

Written by Sharon Gordon

Illustrated by Gioia Fiammenghi

Troll Associates

Library of Congress Cataloging in Publication Data

Gordon, Sharon.
Mike's first haircut.

Summary: Mike is afraid of what he will look like after getting his first haircut.
[1. Haircutting—Fiction] I. Fiammenghi, Gioia, ill. II. Title.
PZ7.G65936Mi 1988 [E] 87-10911
ISBN 0-8167-1113-5 (lib. bdg.)
ISBN 0-8167-1114-3 (pbk.)

Printed in the United States of America.

This is Mike.

Mike's hair is short.

But it grows every day.

It grows longer

and longer.

It grows over his eyes.

It grows over his ears.

Soon, Mike cannot hear.

And Mike cannot see.

"Time for a haircut," says Mother.

“Your hair is too long,” she says.

"A haircut?

Who, me?"

"What will it be?"

"How will it look?"

"Like this? Oh no, please!"

"Like that? Oh no, please!"

"Oh please, not a haircut for me!"

"I would rather not hear.
I would rather not see!"

It was time for a haircut.

Mike's hair was too long.

"What will it be?" asks the man.

"Like this?

Like that?"

"Cut it short," says Mother.

"It grows every day."

"How does it look?" asks the man.

"Is that really *me*?" asks Mike.

"My haircut looks . . . like me!"